You Can Go Home Again

Written and painted
by Jirina Marton

Annick Press
Toronto • New York

©1994 Jirina Marton (text and art)
Cover design by Sheryl Shapiro

Annick Press Ltd.

Annick Press gratefully acknowledges the support of The Canada
Council and the Ontario Arts Council

Canadian Cataloguing in Publication Data

Marton, Jirina
  You can go home again

ISBN 1-55037-991-7 (bound) ISBN 1-55037-990-9 (pbk.)

I. Title.

PS8576.A7943Y6 1994   jC813'.54   C94-930844-7
PZ7.M37Yo 1994

The art in this book was rendered in gouache.
The type was set in Gatineau.

Distributed in Canada by:
Firefly Books Ltd.,
250 Sparks Avenue
Willowdale, ON M2H 2S4

Published in the U.S.A. by Annick Press (U.S.) Ltd.
Distributed in the U.S.A. by:
Firefly Books (U.S.) Inc.
P.O. Box 1338
Ellicott Station
Buffalo, New York 14205

 Printed on acid-free paper.

Printed and bound in Canada by:
D.W. Friesen & Sons, Altona, Manitoba

We have never had a day quite like this before. All afternoon the house was full of people celebrating freedom for my mom's old country. When I went to bed at night, I asked Mom to tell me a story about when she was little.

"Have I ever told you about Aunt Anna and Uncle Billy?" she asked.

"I loved going with my father to see them. The old house was like a fairy-tale setting. There were wonderful smells of old wood, books, spices, teas, and always cake as well.

"The house was full of mysterious things. Nearly all of them were brought back by Uncle Billy from his trips around the world. He was a concert pianist. But the house itself was unusual, too. There was a tiny elevator in one wall and it had a little door with a handle. It made incredible squeaking and rattling noises when food was sent up in it from the kitchen. I always imagined that at night dwarves would ride up and down in it so that they wouldn't have to climb the stairs."

"Did you ever hear Uncle Billy play?"

"Oh, often. Uncle Billy would sit down and play just for me. We would sit on the bench together and play 'four-handed.' My fingers were too short, but I felt so important. He was such a patient teacher.

"But what I loved most were four shiny, dark, wooden elephants made of ebony. They were the only treasures I was allowed to play with... My aunt told lots of stories about them."

"What did you do with them?" I wanted to know.

"Oh, I'd play school with them, or run races with them, or pretend that we were in the jungle. Sometimes I'd show them pictures from books, or I would just put the elephants on the windowsill and look out with them.

"Once I broke the left tusk off the biggest one. I was afraid that I wouldn't be allowed to play with them any more, but Father glued the tusk back on so carefully that you could hardly tell it had been broken."

I couldn't stop thinking about those elephants.

"Where are they now?" I asked Mom at breakfast the next day. She said she didn't know.

"Mom, you promised to finish the story," I said. Dad wanted to hear it, too.

"When the war started," Mom said, "Father, Aunt Anna and Uncle Billy thought I would be safer out of the country. I didn't want to leave them, but I went. I was awfully home-sick."

(Now if this happened to me, I wouldn't go.)

Mom told us that her aunt, her uncle and even her dad died while she was away. Mom stopped. Dad put his hand over hers.

Then I had an idea.

"Maybe we can all go back to your city," I said, "and maybe I could play with those elephants. We could look for them." I thought Dad would say no, but he said it was "a thought worth looking into."

Soon after, we were on our way across the ocean in a big airplane. I wanted to stay awake and watch the clouds from the top, but I was too sleepy.

We landed in the morning and went to a small hotel. All afternoon long we walked through the big city.

We walked and walked. We crossed the river on an old bridge with statues. We visited big old churches.

Mom and Dad took lots of pictures. I took one of Mom and Dad in front of the house Mom lived in when she was small.

We visited the cemetery and went to Mom's old school.

People spoke a different language. They were all the same colour. But the children played hop-scotch like we do.

The buildings were not as high as in Canada, except maybe the churches.

On the second day we went on the subway. I liked the long escalators.

"Where did Aunt and Uncle live? Could we go there?" I asked. Mom and Dad looked at each other, a little surprised. I guessed they had forgotten.

"Oh, dear, the elephants. I have no idea where they could be," Mom said, but we went anyway.

When we finally came to Aunt Anna's and Uncle Billy's house, Mom hardly recognized the place, and I was very disappointed, too. It was so different from what she had told me. The main hallway was dirty. The door to the little elevator was bricked over. Strangers lived there now.

"But have you seen the four elephants?" I asked the tenants. No one seemed to know what I was talking about.

We went to see nice places and people and I liked it all very much, but I kept thinking and asking people about the elephants, and no one had seen them.

I was upset when Dad said we would be leaving the next day. I knew that Mom was sad, too.

"Could we go back to Aunt's and Uncle's house one more time?" I asked. I begged. We went.

The house looked even worse in the dark. I sat down on the sidewalk, and I wanted to cry.

Dad put his hand on my shoulder. "Look, Annie," he said, "we know how important this is to you. The elephants are important to Mom and me as well. But you have done your best, and there just isn't anything else we can do to find them right now. I promise you we won't give up altogether. Let's get a bite to eat now, shall we?"

Right across from the house was a small restaurant. We went in.

That's when it happened. After I finished eating, I looked up. I suddenly noticed something in a glass case on the wall.

"Mom, Dad!" I screamed. "The elephants are here! LOOK!"

The owner of the restaurant came out of the kitchen to see what the commotion was. Mom explained.

He gave Mom a long look and said, "I think I have a story for you."

We looked at him, surprised. I was so excited!

"I met your uncle first," he started. "I used to go to his concerts. Then one day he came here and I discovered that we were neighbours. Sometimes I would go and visit them during the war. Music helped us survive that strange, difficult time.

"The recipe for the dessert you just ate came from your aunt. She and your uncle often talked about you. They were so happy that you were safe.

"After your aunt died, your uncle came every day. He didn't want to be alone. He missed Anna so much... When the war ended, there was a short time of happiness. Then the new government confiscated your uncle's house and everything in it. They let him have just one room to live in.

"One evening he came over here. Under his coat he was carrying these elephants, wrapped in newspaper. He was sure that one day you would come back. So I promised him I would keep them safe for you as long as it would take, but I didn't really believe I would ever meet you!"

Then the owner went and unlocked the glass case and carefully took down the elephants. He set them on the table in front of Mom. She was crying, but I think they were sort of happy tears. She picked up the elephants and looked at them. The biggest had a line of glue on its tusk.

"Oh, Annie," said Mom, "if it hadn't been for you, we wouldn't have found them!" She hugged me, she hugged the owner, and Dad and I did too. We thanked him for everything and promised to come back. He waved to us.

Now, back home, I'm looking at
the elephants. They have a special
place in our house.
We'll never lose them again.

DATE DUE

FE 25

001905